THE CLASSIC TALE

ALICE'S ADVENTURES IN WONDERLAND

From the story by Lewis Carroll

ILLUSTRATED BY GREG HILDEBRANDT

COURAGE
BOOKS
AN IMPRINT OF RUNNING PRESS
PHILADELPHIA • LONDON

9   8   7   6   5   4   3   2   1
Digit on the right indicates the number of this printing

Library of Congress Cataloging-in-Publication Number 2004100541

ISBN 0-7624-2008-1

Cover illustration by Greg Hildebrandt
Cover and Interior Design by Frances J. Soo Ping Chow
Typography: Perpetua, Snell Rounded, and ITC Zapf Dingbats
Text adapted and abridged by Julia Suarez

This book may be ordered by mail from the publisher.
But try your bookstore first!

Published by Courage Books, an imprint of
Running Press Book Publishers
125 South Twenty-second Street
Philadelphia, Pennsylvania 19103-4399

Visit us on the web!
www.runningpress.com

ALICE'S ADVENTURES IN WONDERLAND

ALICE was beginning to get very tired of sitting by her sister on the bank, and of having nothing to do. Once or twice she had peeped into the book her sister was reading, but it had no pictures or conversations in it, 'and what is the use of a book,' thought Alice 'without pictures or conversation?'

So she was considering in her own mind whether the pleasure of making a daisy chain would be worth the trouble of getting up and picking the daisies, when suddenly a White Rabbit with pink eyes ran close by her.

There was nothing so *very* remarkable in that; nor did Alice think it so very much out of the way to hear the Rabbit say to itself, "Oh dear!

Oh dear! I shall be late!" But when the Rabbit actually took a watch out of its waistcoat-pocket, and looked at it, and then hurried on, Alice started to her feet, for it flashed across her mind that she had never before seen a rabbit with either a waistcoat-pocket, or a watch to take out of it, and burning with curiosity, she ran across the field after it and fortunately was just in time to see it pop down a large rabbit hole under the hedge.

In another moment down went Alice after it, never once considering how in the world she was to get out again.

The rabbit-hole went straight on like a tunnel for some ways, and then dipped suddenly down, so suddenly that Alice had not a moment to think about stopping herself before she found herself falling down a very deep well.

Either the well was very deep, or she fell very slowly, for she had plenty of time as she went down to look about her and to wonder what was going to happen next. First, she tried to look down and make out what she was coming to, but it was too dark to see anything. Then she looked at the sides of the well, and noticed that they were filled with cupboards and bookshelves; here and there she saw maps and pictures hung upon pegs.

Down, down, down. There was nothing else to do, so Alice soon began talking. "Dinah'll miss me very much tonight, I should think!" (Dinah was the cat.) "I hope they'll remember her saucer of milk at tea-time." And here Alice began to get rather sleepy. She felt that she was

dozing off, and had just begun to dream when suddenly, down she came upon a heap of sticks and dry leaves, and the fall was over.

Alice was not a bit hurt, and she jumped to her feet in a moment. Before her was another long passage, and the White Rabbit was still in sight, hurrying down it. There was not a moment to be lost: away went Alice like the wind, and was just in time to hear it say, as it turned a corner, "Oh my ears and whiskers, how late it's getting!" She was close behind it when she turned the corner, but the Rabbit was no longer to be seen. She found herself in a long, low hall, which was lit by a row of lamps hanging from the roof.

There were doors all round the hall, but they were all locked; and when Alice had tried every door, she walked sadly down the middle, wondering how she was ever to get out again.

Suddenly she came upon a little three-legged table made of solid glass; there was nothing on it except a tiny golden key, and Alice's first thought was that it might belong to one of the doors of the hall; but, alas! Either the locks were too large, or the key was too small, but at any rate it would not open any of them. However, on the second time round, she came upon a low curtain she had not noticed before, and behind it was a little door about fifteen inches high. She tried the little golden key in the lock, and to her great delight it fitted!

Alice opened the door and found that it led into a small passage. She knelt down and looked along the passage into the loveliest garden you ever saw. How she longed to get out of that dark hall, and wander about among those beds of bright flowers and those cool fountains, but she could not even get her head though the doorway. 'Oh, how I wish I could close up like a telescope!' thought Alice. 'I think I could, if I only knew how to begin.' For, you see, so many out-of-the-way things had happened lately that Alice had begun to think that very few things were really impossible.

There seemed to be no use in waiting by the little door, so she went back to the table. This time she found a little bottle on it, and round the neck of the bottle was a paper label with the words 'DRINK ME' beautifully printed on it in large letters.

It was all very well to say 'DRINK ME,' but wise little Alice was not going to do that in a hurry. "No, I'll look first," she said, "and see whether it's marked 'poison' or not." However, this bottle was not marked 'poison,' so Alice ventured to taste it, and finding it very nice, she very soon finished it off.

"What a curious feeling!" said Alice. "I must be closing up like a telescope."

And so it was indeed. She was now only ten inches high, and her face brightened up at the thought that she was now the right size for going through the little door into that lovely garden. Alas for poor Alice, when she got to the door, she found she had forgotten the little golden key, and when she went back to the table for it, she found she could not possibly reach it.

Soon her eye fell on a little glass box that was lying under the

table. She opened it, and found in it a very small cake, on which the words 'EAT ME' were beautifully marked in currants. She ate a little bit, and she was quite surprised to find that she remained the same size: to be sure, this generally happens when one eats cake, but Alice had got so much into the way of expecting nothing but out-of-the-ordinary things to happen. So she set to work, and very soon finished off the cake.

"Curiouser and curiouser!" cried Alice. "Now I'm opening out like the largest telescope that ever was!" Just then her head struck against the roof of the hall: in fact she was now more than nine feet high, and she at once took up the little golden key and hurried off to the garden door.

Poor Alice! It was as much as she could do, lying down on one side, to look through into the garden with one eye; but to get through was more hopeless than ever and she began to cry.

After a time she heard a little pattering of feet in the distance. It was the White Rabbit returning. With a pair of white kid gloves in one hand and a large fan in the other, he came trotting along in a great hurry, uttering to himself as he came, "Oh! The Duchess! Oh! Won't she be savage if I've kept her waiting!" Alice felt so desperate that she was ready to ask help of anyone, so, when the Rabbit came near her, she began, in a low, timid voice, "If you please, sir—" The Rabbit started violently, dropped the white kid gloves and the fan, and scurried away into the darkness as hard as he could go.

Alice took up the fan and gloves, and, as the hall was very hot, she kept fanning herself all the time she went on talking: "How strange everything is today!" As she said this she looked down at her hands, and was surprised to see that she had put on one of the Rabbit's little white gloves. 'How can I have done that?' she thought. 'I must be growing small again.' She went to the table to measure herself by it, and found that, as nearly as she could guess, she was now about two feet high, and was going on shrinking rapidly. She soon found out that the cause of this was the fan she was holding, and she dropped it hastily, just in time to avoid shrinking away altogether.

"That was a narrow escape!" said Alice, and she ran back to the little door: but, alas! The door was shut again, and the little golden key was lying on the glass table as before, 'and things are worse than ever,' thought the poor child, 'for I never was so small as this before, never!'

As she said these words her foot slipped, and in another moment, splash! She was up to her chin in salt water. Her first idea was that she had somehow fallen into the sea. However, she soon made out that she was in the pool of tears, which she had wept when she was nine feet high.

"I wish I hadn't cried so much!" said Alice, as she swam about, trying to find her way out.

Just then she heard something splashing about in the pool a little way off. At first she thought it must be a walrus or hippopotamus, but then she remembered how small she was now, and she soon made out that it was only a mouse that had slipped in like herself.

'Would it be of any use,' thought Alice, 'to speak to this mouse? Everything is so out-of-the-way down here, that I should think very likely it can talk.' So she began: "O Mouse, do you know the way out of this pool? I am very tired of swimming about here!" The Mouse looked at her rather inquisitively, and seemed to her to wink with one of its little eyes, but it said nothing.

'Perhaps it doesn't understand English,' thought Alice; 'I daresay it's a French mouse.' So she began again: "*Ou est ma chatte?*" which was the first sentence in her French lesson book. The Mouse gave a sudden leap out of the water, and seemed to quiver all over with fright. "Oh, I beg your pardon!" cried Alice hastily, afraid that she had hurt the poor animal's feelings. "I quite forgot you didn't like cats."

"Not like cats!" cried the Mouse, in a shrill, passionate voice. "Would you like cats if you were me?"

"Well, perhaps not," said Alice in a soothing tone. "Don't be angry about it. And yet I wish I could show you our cat Dinah: I think you'd take a fancy to cats if you could only see her. She is such a dear quiet thing," Alice went on, "and she sits purring so nicely by the fire—and she's such a capital one for catching mice—oh, I beg your pardon!" cried Alice. For the mouse was swimming away from her as hard as it could go, and making quite a commotion in the pool as it went.

So she called softly after it, "Mouse dear! Do come back again, and we won't talk about cats, if you don't like them!" When the Mouse heard this, it turned round and swam slowly back to her. Its face was quite pale and it said in a low trembling voice, "Let us get to the shore, and then I'll tell you my history, and you'll understand why it is I hate cats."

It was high time to go, for the pool was getting quite crowded with the birds and animals that had fallen into it: there were a Duck and a Dodo, a Lory and an Eaglet, and several other curious creatures. Alice led the way, and the whole party swam to the shore.

They were indeed a strange-looking party that assembled on the bank—the birds with draggled feathers, the animals with their fur clinging close to them, and all dripping wet, cross, and uncomfortable.

The first question of course was, how to get dry again. They had a consultation about this, and after a few minutes it seemed quite natural to Alice to find herself talking with them, as if she had known them all her life.

At last the Mouse called out, "Sit down, all of you, and listen to me! I'll soon make you dry enough!" They all sat down at once, in a large ring, with the Mouse in the middle. Alice kept her eyes anxiously fixed on it, for she felt sure she would catch a bad cold if she did not get dry soon.

"Ahem!" said the Mouse with an important air, "are you all ready? This is the driest thing I know."

"'William the Conqueror, whose cause was favored by the pope, was soon submitted to by the English, who wanted leaders, and had been of late much accustomed to usurpation and conquest.'"

"How are you getting on now, my dear?" it continued, turning to Alice as it spoke.

"As wet as ever," said Alice in a melancholy tone. "It doesn't seem to dry me at all."

"In that case," said the Dodo solemnly, rising to its feet, "I move that the meeting adjourn for the immediate adoption of more energetic remedies."

"Speak English!" said the Eaglet. "I don't know the meaning of half those long words, and, what's more, I don't believe you do either!"

"What I was going to say," said the Dodo in an offended tone, "was, that the best thing to get us dry would be a Caucus-race."

"What is a Caucus-race?" asked Alice.

"The best way to explain it is to do it," said the Dodo. First it marked out a race course, in a sort of circle and then all the party were placed along the course, here and there. There was no 'One, two, three, and away,' but they began running when they liked, and left off when they liked, so that it was not easy to know when the race was over. However, when they had been running half an hour or so, and were quite dry again, the Dodo suddenly called out "The race is over!" and they all crowded round, panting, and asking, "Who has won?"

This question the Dodo could not answer without a great deal of thought, and it sat for a long time with one finger pressed upon its forehead while the rest waited in silence. At last the Dodo said, "*everybody has won, and all must have prizes.*"

"But who is to give the prizes?" quite a chorus of voices asked.

"Why, she, of course," said the Dodo, pointing to Alice with one finger; and the whole party at once crowded around her, calling out in a confused way, "Prizes! Prizes!"

Alice had no idea what to do, and in despair she put her hand in her pocket, and pulled out a box of comfits and handed them round as prizes. There was exactly one a-piece all round.

"But she must have a prize herself, you know," said the Mouse.

"Of course," the Dodo replied very gravely. "What else have you got in your pocket?" he went on, turning to Alice.

"Only a thimble," said Alice sadly.

"Hand it over here," said the Dodo.

Then they all crowded around her once more, while the Dodo solemnly presented the thimble, saying "We beg your acceptance of this elegant thimble." When it had finished this short speech, they all cheered. Alice thought the whole thing very absurd, but she simply bowed, and took the thimble.

In a little while, Alice again heard a little pattering of footsteps in the distance. It was the White Rabbit, trotting slowly back again, and looking anxiously about as it went as if it had lost something, and she heard it muttering to itself, "The Duchess! Oh my fur and whiskers! She'll get me executed, as sure as ferrets are ferrets! Where can I have dropped them, I wonder?" Alice guessed that it was looking for the fan and the pair of gloves, and she began hunting for them, but they were nowhere to be seen—everything seemed to have changed since her swim in the pool, and the great hall, with the glass table and the little door, had vanished completely.

Very soon the Rabbit noticed Alice and called out to her, "Mary Ann, what are you doing out here? Run home this moment and fetch me a pair of gloves and a fan!" Alice ran off at once in the direction it pointed to, without trying to explain the mistake it had made. 'He took me for his housemaid,' she thought to herself as she ran.

Soon Alice came upon a neat little house, on the door of which was a bright brass plate with the name 'W. Rabbit' engraved upon it. She went in without knocking, and hurried upstairs.

She found her way to a tidy room with a table, and on it (as she had hoped) a fan and two or three pairs of tiny white gloves. She took up the fan and a pair of the gloves, and was just going to leave the room when her eye fell upon a little bottle that stood near the looking-glass. There was no label this time with the words 'DRINK ME' but nevertheless she uncorked it and put it to her lips. 'I know something interesting is sure to happen,' she said to herself, 'so I'll just see what this bottle does. I do hope it'll make me grow large again, for really I'm quite tired of being such a tiny little thing!'

It did so indeed, and much sooner than she had expected. Before she had drunk half the bottle, she found her head pressing against the ceiling, and had to stoop. She hastily put down the bottle, saying to herself, 'That's quite enough—I hope I shan't grow any more—as it is, I can't get out the door!'

Alas, she went on growing, and soon had to kneel on the floor. In another minute there was not even room for this, and she tried the effect of lying down with one elbow against the door, and the other arm curled round her head. Still she went on growing, and as a last resource, she put one arm out of the window, and one foot up the chimney, and said to herself, 'Now I can do no more. What will become of me?'

Luckily for Alice, the little magic bottle had now had its full effect, and she grew no larger. After a few minutes she heard a voice outside, and stopped to listen.

"Mary Ann! Mary Ann!" said the voice. "Fetch me my gloves this moment!" Then came a little pattering of feet on the stairs. Alice knew it was the Rabbit coming to look for her.

Presently, the Rabbit came up to the door and tried to open it; but, as the door opened inwards, and Alice's elbow was pressed hard against it, that attempt proved a failure. Alice heard it say to itself, "Then I'll go round and get in at the window."

'That you won't' thought Alice, and after waiting till she fancied she heard the Rabbit just under the window, she suddenly spread out her hand and made a snatch in the air. She did not get hold of anything, but she heard a little shriek and a fall, and a crash of broken glass.

Next came an angry voice—the Rabbit's—"Pat! Pat! Where are you?" And then a voice she had never heard before, "Sure then I'm here!"

"Now tell me, Pat, what's that in the window?"

"It's an arm, yer honour!"

"Well, it's got no business there. Go and take it away!"

There was a long silence after this and she waited for some time without hearing anything more. At last came a rumbling of little cartwheels, and the sound of a good many voices all talking together. She made out the words, "Bill! The master says you're to go down the chimney!"

'So Bill's got to come down the chimney, has he?' said Alice to herself. 'I wouldn't be in Bill's place. This fireplace is narrow, but I think I can kick a little!'

She drew her foot as far down the chimney as she could, and waited till she heard a little animal scratching and scrambling about in the chimney close above her. Then, she gave one sharp kick, and waited to see what would happen next.

The first thing she heard was a general chorus of, "There goes Bill!" Then the Rabbit's voice—"Catch him!" then silence, and then another confusion of voices—"What happened to you? Tell us all about it!"

At last came a little squeaking voice. "Well, I hardly know—all I know is, something comes at me like a Jack-in-the-box, and up I goes like a sky-rocket!"

"So you did, old fellow!" said the others.

"We must burn the house down!" said the Rabbit's voice, and Alice called out as loud as she could, "If you do. I'll set Dinah on you!"

There was a dead silence instantly. After a minute or two, Alice heard the Rabbit say, "A barrowful will do, to begin with."

"A barrowful of what?" thought Alice; but she had not long to doubt, for the next moment a shower of little pebbles came rattling in the window and some of them hit her in the face. 'I'll put a stop to this,' she said to herself, and shouted out, "You'd better not do that again!" which produced another dead silence.

Alice noticed with some surprise that the pebbles were all turning into little cakes as they lay on the floor, and a bright idea came into her head. 'If I eat one of these cakes,' she thought, 'it's sure to make some change in my size; and as it can't possibly make me larger, it must make me smaller.'

So she swallowed one of the cakes, and was delighted to find that she began shrinking. As soon as she was small enough, she ran out of the house and found a crowd of little animals and birds waiting outside. They all made a rush at Alice the moment she appeared; but she ran off as hard as she could and soon found herself safe in a thick wood.

'The first thing I've got to do,' said Alice to herself, 'is to grow to my right size again; and the second thing is to find my way into that lovely garden. I think that will be the best plan.'

While she was peering about anxiously among the trees, a sharp bark over her head made her look up in a great hurry.

An enormous puppy was looking down at her with large round eyes, stretching out one paw, trying to touch her. Alice tried hard to

whistle to it, but she was terribly frightened that it might be hungry, in which case it would be very likely to eat her up.

Hardly knowing what she did, she picked up a little bit of stick and held it out to the puppy; the puppy jumped into the air off all its feet at once, and with a yelp of delight, rushed at the stick. Then the puppy began a series of short charges at the stick, till at last it sat down a good way off, with its tongue hanging out of its mouth and its great eyes half shut.

This seemed to Alice a good opportunity for making her escape, so she set off at once running until she was quite tired and out of breath, and till the puppy's bark sounded quite faint in the distance.

"What a dear little puppy it was!" said Alice, as she leant against a buttercup to rest herself. "I should have liked teaching it tricks—if I'd only been the right size to do it! Oh dear! I'd nearly forgotten that I've got to grow up again! I suppose I ought to eat or drink something or other, but the great question is, what?"

The great question certainly was, what? Alice looked all round her at the flowers and the blades of grass, but she did not see anything that looked like the right thing to eat or drink under the circumstances. There was a large mushroom growing near her, about the same height as herself. She stretched herself up on tiptoe, and peeped over the edge of it. Her eyes immediately met those of a large caterpillar that was sitting on the top with its arms folded, quietly smoking a long hookah, and taking not the smallest notice of her or of anything else.

The Caterpillar and Alice looked at each other for some time in silence: until at last the Caterpillar took the hookah out of its mouth and addressed her in a languid, sleepy voice.

"Who are you?" said the Caterpillar.

Alice replied, rather shyly, "I—I hardly know, sir, just at present— at least I know who I was when I got up this morning, but I think I must have been changed several times since then."

"What do you mean by that?" said the Caterpillar sternly. "Explain yourself!"

"I can't explain myself, I'm afraid, sir," said Alice, "because I'm not myself, you see."

"I don't see," said the Caterpillar.

"I'm afraid I can't put it more clearly," Alice replied very politely, "for I can't understand it myself; and being so many different sizes in a day is very confusing."

"It isn't," said the Caterpillar.

"Well, perhaps you haven't found it so yet," said Alice. "But when you have to turn into a chrysalis and then after that into a butterfly, I should think you'll feel it a little strange, won't you?"

"Not a bit," said the Caterpillar.

"Well, perhaps your feelings may be different," said Alice. "All I know is, it would feel very strange to me."

For some minutes the Caterpillar puffed away without speaking, but at last it took the hookah out of its mouth again, and said, "So you think you're changed, do you? What size do you want to be?"

"Oh, I'm not particular as to size," Alice hastily replied. "Only one doesn't like changing so often, you know."

"I don't know," said the Caterpillar. Alice said nothing; she had never been so much contradicted in her life before, and she felt that she was losing her temper. "Are you content now?" said the caterpillar.

"Well, I should like to be a little larger, sir, if you wouldn't mind," said Alice. "Three inches is such a wretched height to be."

"It is a very good height indeed!" said the Caterpillar angrily, rearing itself upright as it spoke (it was exactly three inches high).

"But I'm not used to it!" pleaded poor Alice in a piteous tone.

"You'll get used to it in time," said the Caterpillar, and it put the hookah into its mouth and began smoking again.

This time Alice waited patiently. In a minute or two the Caterpillar got down off the mushroom, and crawled away in the grass, merely remarking as it went, "One side will make you grow taller, and the other side will make you grow shorter."

'One side of what? The other side of what?' thought Alice to herself.

"Of the mushroom," said the Caterpillar, just as if she had asked it aloud; and in another moment it was out of sight.

Alice looked thoughtfully at the mushroom for a minute, trying to make out which were the two sides of it. At last she stretched her arms round it as far as they would go, and broke off a bit of the edge with each hand.

'And now which is which?' she said to herself, and nibbled a little of the right-hand bit to try the effect. The next moment she was shrinking rapidly, so she set to work at once to eat some of the other bit.

It was so long since she had been anything near the right size that it felt quite strange at first; but she got used to it in a few minutes, and began talking to herself, as usual. 'There's half my plan done now! How puzzling all these changes are! However, I've got back to my right size. The next thing is to get into that beautiful garden—how is that to be done, I wonder?' As she said this, she came suddenly upon an open place, with a little house in it about four feet high. 'Whoever lives there,' thought Alice, 'it'll never do to come upon them this size. Why, I should frighten them out of their wits!' So she began nibbling at the right hand bit again and did not venture to go near the house till she had brought herself down to nine inches high.

Suddenly a footman in livery came running out of the wood— judging by his face only, she would have called him a fish—and rapped loudly at the door with his knuckles. It was opened by another foot-man in livery, with a round face and large eyes like a frog. Both footmen, Alice noticed, had powdered hair that curled all over their heads.

The Fish-Footman began by producing from under his arm a great letter, nearly as large as himself, saying in a solemn tone, "For the Duchess. An invitation from the Queen to play croquet." The Frog-Footman repeated, in the same solemn tone, only changing the order

of the words a little, "From the Queen. An invitation for the Duchess to play croquet." Then they both bowed low, and their curls got entangled together.

Alice laughed so much at this that she had to run back into the wood for fear of their hearing her; when she next peeped out, the Fish-Footman was gone, and the other was sitting on the ground near the door.

Alice went timidly up to the door and knocked. At this moment, the door of the house opened and a large plate came skimming out, straight at the Footman's head. It grazed his nose and broke to pieces against one of the trees behind him.

The door led right into a large kitchen, which was full of smoke from one end to the other. The Duchess was sitting on a three-legged stool in the middle, nursing a baby; the cook was leaning over the fire, stirring a cauldron full of soup.

'There's certainly too much pepper in that soup!' Alice said to herself, as well as she could for sneezing.

There was certainly too much of it in the air. Even the Duchess sneezed occasionally and as for the baby, it was sneezing and howling alternately without a moment's pause. The only things in the kitchen that did not sneeze were the cook and a large cat, which was sitting on the hearth and grinning from ear to ear.

"Would you tell me," asked Alice, "why your cat grins like that?"

"It's a Cheshire cat," said the Duchess.

"I didn't know that Cheshire cats always grinned; in fact, I didn't know that cats could grin," said Alice.

"You don't know much," said the Duchess, "and that's a fact."

Alice did not like the tone of this remark and thought it would be as well to introduce some other subject of conversation. While she was trying to fix on one, the cook took the cauldron of soup off the fire, and at once set to work throwing everything within her reach at the Duchess and the baby.

"Oh, please mind what you're doing!" cried Alice, jumping up and down in an agony of terror.

"Here! You may nurse it a bit, if you like!" the Duchess said to Alice, flinging the baby at her as she spoke. "I must go and get ready to play croquet with the Queen," and she hurried out of the room.

Alice caught the baby with some difficulty, as it was a queer-shaped little creature, and held out its arms and legs in all directions. The poor little thing was snorting like a steam-engine when she caught it, and kept doubling itself up and straightening itself out again, so that it was as much as she could do to hold it. The baby grunted, and Alice looked very anxiously into its face to see what was the matter with it. There could be no doubt that it had a very turned-up nose, much more like a snout than a real nose; also its eyes were extremely small for a baby. Alice did not like the look of the thing at all.

"If you're going to turn into a pig," said Alice seriously, "I'll have nothing more to do with you." The creature grunted again, so violently

that she looked down into its face in some alarm. This time there could be no mistake about it: it was neither more nor less than a pig, so she set the little creature down and felt quite relieved to see it trot away quietly into the wood. 'If it had grown up,' she said to herself, 'it would have made a dreadfully ugly child. But it makes rather a handsome pig, I think.'

Alice looked up and was a little startled to see the Cheshire Cat sitting on a bough of a tree a few yards off. The Cat only grinned when it saw Alice. It looked good-natured, she thought. Still, it had very long claws and a great many teeth, so she felt that it ought to be treated with respect.

"Cheshire Puss," she began, rather timidly, as she did not at all know whether it would like the name. "Would you tell me, please, which way I ought to go from here?"

"That depends a good deal on where you want to get to," said the Cat.

"I don't much care where—" said Alice.

"Then it doesn't matter which way you go," said the Cat.

"—so long as I get somewhere," Alice added as an explanation.

"Oh, you're sure to do that," said the Cat, "if you only walk long enough."

Alice felt that this could not be denied, so she tried another question. "What sort of people live here?"

"In that direction," the Cat said, waving its right paw round, "lives a Hatter. And in that direction," waving the other paw, "lives a March Hare. They're both mad."

"But I don't want to go among mad people," Alice remarked.

"Oh, you can't help that. We're all mad here." said the Cat, and vanished.

Alice was not much surprised at this. After a minute or two she walked on in the direction in which the March Hare was said to live.

She had not gone much farther before she came in sight of the house of the March Hare. She thought it must be the right house because the chimneys were shaped like ears and the roof was thatched with fur. There was a table set out under a tree in front of the house and the March Hare and the Hatter were having tea at it; a Dormouse was sitting between them, fast asleep. The table was a large one, but the three were all crowded together at one corner of it. "No room! No room!" they cried out when they saw Alice coming.

"There's plenty of room!" said Alice indignantly, and she sat down in a large chair at one end of the table.

The Hatter opened his eyes very wide on hearing this but all he said was, "Why is a raven like a writing-desk?"

"I believe I can guess that," said Alice.

"Do you mean that you think you can find out the answer to it?" said the March Hare.

"Exactly so," said Alice.

"Then you should say what you mean," the March Hare went on.

"I do," Alice hastily replied; "at least I mean what I say—that's the same thing."

"Not the same thing at all!" said the Hatter. "You might just as well say that 'I see what I eat' is the same thing as 'I eat what I see!'"

"You might just as well say," added the March Hare, "that 'I like what I get' is the same thing as 'I get what I like!'" Here the conversation dropped and the party sat silent for a minute while Alice thought over all she could remember about ravens and writing-desks, which wasn't much.

The Hatter was the first to break the silence. "What day of the month is it?" he said turning to Alice. He had taken his watch out of his pocket and was looking at it uneasily, shaking it every now and then, and holding it to his ear.

Alice considered a little, and then said, "The fourth."

"Two days wrong!" sighed the Hatter.

Alice had been looking over his shoulder with some curiosity. "What a funny watch!" she remarked. "It tells the day of the month and doesn't tell what o'clock it is!"

"Why should it?" muttered the Hatter. "Does your watch tell you what year it is?"

"Of course not," Alice replied. "But that's because it stays the same year for such a long time."

"Which is just the case with mine," said the Hatter.

Alice felt dreadfully puzzled. The Hatter's remark seemed to have no sort of meaning in it and yet it was certainly English. "I don't quite understand you," she said, as politely as she could.

"Have you guessed the riddle yet?" the Hatter said, turning to Alice again.

"No, I give it up," Alice replied. "What's the answer?"

"I haven't the slightest idea," said the Hatter.

Alice sighed wearily. "I think you might do something better with the time," she said, "than waste it in asking riddles that have no answers."

"If you knew Time as well as I do," said the Hatter, "you wouldn't talk about wasting it. It's him."

"I don't know what you mean," said Alice.

"Of course you don't!" the Hatter said. "I dare say you never even spoke to Time!"

"Perhaps not," Alice replied. "But I know I have to beat time when I learn music."

"Ah! That accounts for it," said the Hatter. "Now, if you only kept on good terms with him, he'd do almost anything you liked with the clock. For instance, suppose it were nine o'clock in the morning, just time to begin lessons. You'd only have to whisper a hint to Time and round goes the clock in a twinkling! Half-past one, time for dinner!"

"That would be grand, certainly," said Alice thoughtfully. "But then—I shouldn't be hungry for it, you know."

"Not at first, perhaps," said the Hatter. "But you could keep it to half-past one as long as you liked."

"Is that the way you manage?" Alice asked.

The Hatter shook his head mournfully. "Not I!" he replied. "We quarreled last March and ever since he won't do a thing I ask! It's always six o'clock now."

A bright idea came into Alice's head. "Is that the reason so many tea things are put out here?" she asked.

"Yes, that's it," said the Hatter with a sigh. "It's always tea time, and we've no time to wash the things between whiles."

"Then you keep moving round, I suppose?" said Alice.

"Exactly so," said the Hatter. "As the things get used up."

"But what happens when you come to the beginning again?" Alice ventured to ask.

"Suppose we change the subject," the March Hare interrupted, yawning. "Take some more tea," he said to Alice.

"I've had nothing yet," Alice replied in an offended tone, "so I can't take more."

"You mean you can't take less," said the Hatter. "It's very easy to take more than nothing."

Alice did not quite know what to say to this so she helped herself to some tea and bread and butter.

"I want a clean cup," interrupted the Hatter. "Let's all move one place on."

He moved on as he spoke and the Dormouse followed him. The March Hare moved into the Dormouse's place and Alice rather unwillingly took the place of the March Hare. The Hatter was the only one who got any advantage from the change and Alice was a good deal worse off than before, as the March Hare had just upset the milk jug into his plate.

This piece of rudeness was more than Alice could bear. She got up in disgust and walked off. "I'll never go there again!" said Alice as she picked her way through the wood. "It's the stupidest tea party I ever was at in all my life!"

Just as she said this, she noticed that one of the trees had a door leading right into it. 'That's very curious!' she thought. 'But everything's curious today. I think I may as well go in.' And in she went.

Once more she found herself in the long hall close to the little glass table. 'I'll manage better this time,' she said to herself, and began by taking the little golden key and unlocking the door that led into the garden. Then she nibbled at the mushroom (she had kept a piece of it in her pocket) till she was about a foot high. Then she walked down the little passage, and found herself at last in the beautiful garden.

A large rose tree stood near the entrance of the garden. The roses growing on it were white but there were three gardeners busily painting them red. Just as she came up to them she heard one of them say, "Look out now, Five! Don't go splashing paint over me like that!"

"You'd better not talk, Seven!" said Five. "I heard the Queen say only yesterday you deserved to be beheaded!"

Seven flung down his brush, and had just begun "Well, of all

the unjust things—" when his eye chanced to fall upon Alice and he checked himself suddenly. The others looked round also, and all of them bowed low.

"Would you tell me," said Alice, a little timidly, "why you are painting those roses?"

Two began in a low voice, "Why you see, Miss, this here ought to have been a red rose tree. We put a white one in by mistake and if the Queen was to find out, we should all have our heads cut off." At this moment Five called out, "The Queen! The Queen!" and the three gardeners threw themselves flat upon their faces. There was a sound of many footsteps, and Alice looked round, eager to see the Queen.

First came ten soldiers carrying clubs; next ten courtiers ornamented all over with diamonds. After these came the royal children; there were ten of them, and they were all ornamented with hearts. Next came the guests and among them Alice recognized the White Rabbit. Last of all came the King and Queen of hearts.

When the procession came to Alice they all stopped and looked at her, and the Queen said severely, "What's your name, child?"

"My name is Alice," said Alice very politely; but she added, to herself, 'Why, they're only a pack of cards. I needn't be afraid of them!'

"Can you play croquet?" asked the Queen.

"Yes!" said Alice.

"Come on, then!" roared the Queen, and Alice joined the procession.

"It's a very fine day!" said a timid voice at her side. She was walking by the White Rabbit, who was peeping anxiously into her face.

"Very," said Alice. "Where's the Duchess?"

"Hush!" said the Rabbit in a low, hurried tone. He looked anxiously over his shoulder as he spoke, and then raised himself upon tiptoe, put his mouth close to her ear, and whispered, "She's under sentence of execution."

"Get to your places!" shouted the Queen in a voice of thunder and people began running about in all directions; they got settled down in a minute or two, and the game began. Alice thought she had never seen such a curious croquet-ground in her life; the balls were live hedgehogs, the mallets live flamingoes, and the soldiers had to double themselves up and stand on their hands and feet to make the arches.

The chief difficulty Alice found at first was in managing her flamingo. She succeeded in getting its body tucked away under her arm, with its legs hanging down. But just as she had got its neck nicely straightened out, and was going to give the hedgehog a blow with its head, it would twist itself round and look up in her face, with such a puzzled expression that she could not help bursting out laughing. And when she had got its head down, and was going to begin again, she found that the hedgehog had unrolled itself, and was in the act of crawling away. The players all played at once without waiting for turns, and in a very short time the Queen was in a furious passion and went stamping about, shouting, 'Off with his head!' or 'Off with her head!' about once in a minute.

Alice began to feel very uneasy. She had not as yet had any dispute with the Queen, but she knew that it might happen at any minute. 'They're dreadfully fond of beheading people here,' thought Alice. 'The great wonder is, that there's anyone left alive!'

She was looking about for some way of escape, and wondering whether she could get away without being seen, when she noticed a curious appearance in the air. She made it out to be a grin, and she said to herself 'It's the Cheshire Cat.'

"How do you like the queen?" said the Cat, as soon as there was mouth enough for it to speak with.

"Not at all," said Alice. "She's so extremely—" Just then she noticed that the Queen was close behind her, listening. So she went on, "—likely to win, that it's hardly worth while finishing the game."

The Queen smiled and passed on.

"Who are you talking to?" said the King, going up to Alice, and looking at the Cat with great curiosity.

"It's a friend of mine—a Cheshire Cat," said Alice. "Allow me to introduce it."

"I don't like the look of it at all. It must be removed," said the King very decidedly, and he called the Queen, who was passing at the moment. "My dear! I wish you would have this cat removed!"

The Queen had only one way of settling all difficulties, great or small. "Off with his head!" she said, without even looking around.

"I'll fetch the executioner myself," said the King eagerly, and he hurried off.

Alice thought she might as well go back and see how the game was going on, so she went in search of her hedgehog. When she got back to the Cheshire Cat, she was surprised to find quite a large crowd collected round it. There was a dispute going on between the executioner, the King, and the Queen, who were all talking at once.

The moment Alice appeared, she was appealed to by all three to settle the question, and they repeated their arguments to her. Alice could think of nothing else to say but "It belongs to the Duchess, you'd better ask her about it."

"She's in prison," the Queen said to the executioner. "Fetch her here." And the executioner went off like an arrow.

The Cat's head began fading away the moment he was gone, and, by the time he had come back with the Duchess, it had entirely disappeared; so the King and the executioner ran wildly up and down looking for it, while the rest of the party went back to the game.

"You can't think how glad I am to see you again!" said the Duchess, as she tucked her arm into Alice's and they walked off together.

Alice was very glad to find her in such a pleasant temper. "The game's going rather better now," she said, by way of keeping up the conversation a little.

" 'Tis so," said the Duchess, "and the moral of that is—'tis love, 'tis love, that makes the world go round!'"

"Somebody said," Alice whispered, "that it's done by everybody minding their own business!"

"Ah, well! It means much the same thing," said the Duchess as she added, "and the mora——"

But here, to Alice's great surprise, the Duchess's voice died away in the middle of her favorite word 'moral,' and the arm that was linked into hers began to tremble. Alice looked up, and there stood the Queen in front of them.

"A fine day, your Majesty!" the Duchess began in a low, weak voice.

"I give you fair warning," shouted the Queen, stamping on the ground as she spoke. "Either you or your head must be off! Take your choice!"

The Duchess took her choice and was gone in a moment.

"Let's go on with the game," the Queen said to Alice, and Alice was too much frightened to say a word, but slowly followed her back to the croquet-ground.

All the time they were playing, the Queen never left off quarrelling with the other players and shouting "Off with his head!" or "Off with her head!" Those whom she sentenced were taken into custody by the soldiers who, of course, had to leave off being arches to do this, so that by the end of half an hour there were no arches left, and all the players, except the King, the Queen, and Alice, were in custody and under sentence of execution.

Then the Queen said to Alice, "Have you seen the Mock Turtle yet?"

"No," said Alice. "I don't even know what a Mock Turtle is."

"Come on, then," said the Queen, "and he shall tell you his history."

They very soon came upon a Gryphon, lying fast asleep in the sun.

"Up, lazy thing!" said the Queen, "and take this young lady to see the Mock Turtle, and to hear his history. I must go back and see after some executions I have ordered," and she walked off, leaving Alice alone with the Gryphon.

The Gryphon sat up and rubbed its eyes. It watched the Queen till she was out of sight, then it chuckled. "What fun!" said the Gryphon.

"What is the fun?" asked Alice.

"Why, it's all her fancy," said the Gryphon. "They never execute anybody, you know. Come on!"

So they went up to the Mock Turtle, who looked at them with large eyes full of tears, but said nothing.

"This here young lady," said the Gryphon, "she wants for to know your history, she do."

"I'll tell it her," said the Mock Turtle in a deep, hollow tone. "Sit down, both of you, and don't speak a word till I've finished."

"Once," said the Mock Turtle with a deep sigh, "I was a real Turtle. When we were little, we went to school in the sea. The master was an old Turtle—we used to call him Tortoise—"

"Why did you call him Tortoise, if he wasn't one?" Alice asked.

"We called him Tortoise because he taught us," said the Mock

Turtle angrily. "Really, you are very dull!" And he went on: "Yes, we went to school in the sea, though you mayn't believe it—"

"I never said I didn't!" interrupted Alice.

"You did," said the Mock Turtle. "We had the best of educations—in fact, we went to school every day—"

"And how many hours a day did you do lessons?" said Alice.

"Ten hours the first day," said the Mock Turtle. "Nine the next, and so on."

"What a curious plan!" exclaimed Alice.

This was quite a new idea to Alice, and she thought it over a little before she made her next remark. "Then the eleventh day must have been a holiday."

"Of course it was," said the Mock Turtle.

"And how did you manage on the twelfth?" Alice went on eagerly.

"That's enough about lessons," the Gryphon interrupted in a very decided tone.

"Oh, a song, please, if the Mock Turtle would be so kind," Alice replied, so eagerly that the Gryphon said, "Sing her "Turtle Soup," will you, old fellow?"

The Mock Turtle sighed deeply, and began to sing this:

"Beautiful Soup, so rich and green,

Waiting in a hot tureen!

Who for such dainties would not stoop?

Soup of the evening, beautiful Soup!

Soup of the evening, beautiful Soup!

Beau—ootiful Soo—oop!

Beau—ootiful Soo—oop!

Soo—oop of the e—e—evening,

Beautiful, beautiful Soup!

"Chorus again!" cried the Gryphon, and the Mock Turtle had just begun to repeat it, when a cry of "The trial's beginning!" was heard in the distance.

"Come on!" cried the Gryphon, and taking Alice by the hand, it hurried off, without waiting for the end of the song.

"What trial is it?" Alice panted as she ran; but the Gryphon only answered "Come on!" and ran faster.

The King and Queen of Hearts were seated on their thrones when they arrived. A great crowd was assembled about them and the Knave was standing before them, in chains, with a soldier on each side to guard him. Near the King was the White Rabbit, with a trumpet in one hand, and a scroll of parchment in the other. In the very middle of the court was a table, with a large dish of tarts upon it. They looked so good that it made Alice quite hungry to look at them. 'I wish they'd get the trial done,' she thought, 'and hand round the refreshments!' But there seemed to be no chance of this, so she began looking at everything about her to pass the time.

The judge was the King. The twelve jurors were all writing very busily on slates.

"Herald, read the accusation!" said the King.

The White Rabbit blew three blasts on the trumpet and then unrolled the parchment scroll and read as follows:

"The Queen of Hearts, she made some tarts,

All on a summer day.

The Knave of Hearts, he stole those tarts,

And took them quite away!"

"Call the first witness," said the King and the White Rabbit blew three blasts on the trumpet and called out, "First witness!"

The first witness was the Hatter. He came in with a teacup in one hand and a piece of bread and butter in the other. "I beg pardon, your Majesty," he began, "for bringing these in but I hadn't quite finished my tea when I was sent for."

"Give your evidence," said the King "and don't be nervous, or I'll have you executed on the spot."

This did not seem to encourage the witness at all. He kept shifting from one foot to the other looking uneasily at the Queen. In his confusion, he bit a large piece out of his teacup instead of the bread and butter.

Just at this moment Alice felt a very curious sensation. She was beginning to grow larger again, and she thought at first she would get up and leave the court but on second thoughts she decided to remain where she was as long as there was room for her.

"Give your evidence," the King repeated angrily, "or I'll have you executed, whether you're nervous or not."

The miserable Hatter dropped his teacup and bread and butter and went down on one knee. "I'm a poor man, your Majesty," he began.

"You're a very poor speaker," said the King. "If that's all you know about it, you may stand down."

"I can't go no lower," said the Hatter. "I'm on the floor, as it is."

"You may go," said the King and the Hatter hurriedly left the court.

"Call the next witness!" said the King.

Alice watched the White Rabbit as he fumbled over the list, feeling very curious to see what the next witness would be like, '—for they haven't got much evidence yet,' she said to herself. Imagine her surprise, when the White Rabbit read out, at the top of his shrill little voice, the name "Alice!"

"Here!" cried Alice.

"What do you know about this business?" the King said to Alice.

"Nothing," said Alice.

At this moment the King, who had been busily writing in his notebook, cackled out "Silence!" and read out from his book, "Rule Forty-two. All persons more than a mile high must leave the court."

Everybody looked at Alice.

"That's not a regular rule. You invented it just now," said Alice.

"It's the oldest rule in the book," said the King.

"Then it ought to be Number One," said Alice.

"Off with her head!" the Queen shouted at the top of her voice.

"Who cares for you?" said Alice (she had grown to her full size by this time). "You're nothing but a pack of cards!"

At this the whole pack rose up into the air, and came flying down upon her. She tried to beat them off, and found herself lying on her back, with her head in the lap of her sister, who was gently brushing away some dead leaves that had fluttered down from the trees upon her face.

"Wake up, Alice dear!" said her sister. "Why, what a long sleep you've had!"

"Oh, I've had such a curious dream!" said Alice. She told her sister, as well as she could remember, all these strange Adventures of hers that you have just been reading about, and when she had finished, her sister kissed her, and said, "It was a curious dream, dear, certainly, but now run in to your tea; it's getting late." So Alice got up and ran off, thinking while she ran, as well she might, what a wonderful dream it had been.

THE END